To friends everywhere

JANETTA OTTER-BARRY BOOKS

First published in Great Britain and in the USA in 2013
by Frances Lincoln Children's Books,
74-77 White Lion Street, London N1 9PF
www.franceslincoln.com

British Library Cataloguing in Publication Data available on request

ISBN 978-1-84780-317-7

Illustrated with acrylic

Set in Bokka-Solid

Printed in Dongguan, Guangdong, China by Toppan Leefung in March, 2013

1 3 5 7 9 8 6 4 2

# Lenny GOes to Nursery School

## Ken Wilson-Max

F
FRANCES LINCOLN
CHILDREN'S BOOKS

Here's Lenny, on his way to nursery school with Mummy.

It's his first day at school.
Lenny is excited but a bit afraid.

At the school gate Lenny sees
a girl with colourful clothes.

Lenny points and smiles.

They all go inside and the girl says goodbye to her mum.

"Bye bye, Lucy," says her mum.
The girl waves back.

Mummy says, "Bye bye, Lenny. See you later."
Lenny frowns and waves a little wave.

Lucy takes Lenny's hand.
"Let's play," she says.

The teacher asks the children to sit next to a partner.

Lenny sits next to Lucy.

The class sing a song together.

The wheels on the bus
Go round and round...

At break-time, Lenny and Lucy drink some juice.

They draw pictures of each other
and colour the pictures in.

They play 'Follow the Leader'
with the tricycles...

and then they play catch
with the big ball.

Then it's time for a story.

At the end of the first day
at nursery school Mummy
comes to fetch Lenny.
She gives him a big hug.
Lenny hugs her back.

Lenny and Lucy play a little while
longer until Lucy's mum arrives.

Lucy and Lenny say,
"Bye bye. See you tomorrow."